This book belongs to

. . . .

The Christmas Story as told by
Assellus
the Christmas Donkey

Janet Duggan

Illustrated by Catherine Robertson

The Christmas Story as told by
Assellus the Christmas Donkey

Written by Janet Duggan

Illustrated by Catherine Robertson

Copyright © Janet Duggan 2009

All rights reserved. No part of this publication may be reproduced, stored in a retrieval system or transmitted in any form or by any means electronic, mechanical, audio, visual or otherwise, without prior permission of the copyright owner. Nor can it be circulated in any form of binding or cover other than that in which it is published and without similar conditions including this condition being imposed on the subsequent purchaser. Every effort has been made to seek copyright permission for quotations and illustrations published in this book; any omissions are regretted and can be rectified immediately.

ISBN: 978-0-9563389-0-7

Published by Janet Duggan
in conjunction with Writersworld Ltd

Printed and bound by www.printondemand-worldwide.com

Copy edited by Jeremy Renals

www.writersworld.co.uk

WRITERSWORLD
2 Bear Close
Woodstock
Oxfordshire
OX20 1JX
United Kingdom

This book is dedicated to Emma and Matthew

"Thank goodness for that! Here comes my supper at last!

It's so late that I really thought my master had forgotten me this evening. Can you hear my tummy rumbling?

Oh, I'm sorry, you don't even know who I am yet. Silly me!

Let me introduce myself; my name is Assellus and I am a grey donkey.

I am centuries old, and I expect to live forever because I live in a timeless village called Nazareth. It is a small village filled with small, white flat-roofed houses. From a distance they remind me of the many sheep we have in this area, who also cluster on the hillside.

I must tell you about the lady and man to whom I belong; Mary and Joseph.

Mary is young, with dark hair, a fresh face and large brown eyes. Here she is with Joseph. Do you like her long blue dress? Mary is quiet, kind and gentle; always serene.

At the moment she has a fat tummy because she is going to have a baby - her very first! I think I am almost as excited about it as Mary and Joseph are!

Joseph is older than Mary and has long, thick hair and a thick beard. He is a carpenter. You should see his wonderful tools! Give Joseph a piece of wood and what he can't make out of it isn't worth making, I can tell you!

There are many donkeys like me around here, as people don't have cars. We are used as vehicles to move people and goods around.

I know I am more than just transport to Mary and Joseph though; I am also their pet and their friend. I know this because they chatter to me quite often. I am glad I am their donkey; they treat me as a being with feelings. Not like some of our neighbours who kick and beat their donkeys but never talk to them.

Mary and Joseph are not very rich with money, but they are very rich with love, good qualities and happiness.

Yes, well, having mentioned happiness, I must admit that Joseph did not look very happy just now when he brought in my supper. He has something on his mind.

What can it be?

Perhaps it is something to do with the baby. Listen! Mary has just returned from visiting her cousin, Elizabeth. Joseph has rushed out to meet her, looking anxious, with a letter in his hand. If I bend my ear, I'll be able to catch what they say, then I can tell you.

Oh no! It's about the Emperor who rules this country. It seems that he has ordered all citizens to go back to the town where they were born to be counted and taxed, which means I suppose, that they will have to pay out some money.

Mary is looking distressed – I can't say I blame her, she could do without going on any long journeys in her condition! I don't really fancy the idea of a long journey myself. I am quite content to potter around the streets of Nazareth or munch the grass and watch the world go by. Still, if we are going, I had better have an early night.

See you in the morning when it's dawning!

Who's that stroking my head? It's Joseph! Surely, it's not morning already. Oh yes - today's the day we are off on our long, unwanted journey. Joseph is explaining to me that we will be on the road a long time before we reach Bethlehem; the city of his ancestors.

Here comes Mary. She has a bundle which she is strapping to my back. No doubt the bundle contains clothes for the baby, in case it is born in Bethlehem.

Joseph is waiting to lead me off - I'll just finish drinking this water he brought me fresh from the well. That's better. Now, off we go - I wonder what adventures lie ahead of us?

Oh my poor, aching hooves! We've been walking for miles and miles. I've slowed down a lot and I feel I cannot go much further. My head feels light and peculiar but the rest of my body feels as heavy as a sack of stones.

Mary has been riding on me for the past few miles; Joseph insisted, though she didn't want to because she felt it would be too much for me. It almost is too!

But I won't complain because Mary is so sweet and good. I will keep going until I collapse if it helps her. Even though I am bearing a great burden I am pleased to be able to return Mary's kindness. Does it make you feel good too, when you are able to return kindness to those who have been kind to you?

I am walking very carefully so as not to give Mary any sudden jolts - I wouldn't want to be responsible for making her baby be born on the journey!

I can't believe my eyes! Is that really Bethlehem over there? Joseph says it is - what a relief! You have no idea how weary my poor, old bones are!

Keep going Assellus. Not far now. Keep going! I am afraid I am always talking to myself like this.

It has been so very hot today and the dust from the roads has got into my throat. I could drain the River Jordan dry. Poor Mary and Joseph look tired too. Joseph is dragging his feet along. What a dusty trio we make - now entering Bethlehem!

Goodness me! What crowds! I've never seen so many people, all milling about in the streets; all here for the same purpose. I suppose I should have expected it but somehow I didn't.

Joseph is trying to book a room for the night at the city's main inn but the innkeeper is shaking his head, so we are having to look elsewhere. What about this place? No? This place is full too, in fact, the innkeeper says he has crammed in far more people than he can comfortably manage already.

Oh dear, that's not very encouraging, is it? Joseph is trying the last inn. Keep your fingers crossed! Oh, he is looking very worried - I can't bear to hear it! What will we do now? Night is falling fast, as it does in this part of the world; soon it will become very, very cold.

Oh, that inn is full to overflowing as well. Joseph is pointing to his wife, explaining that she must have somewhere to rest. The inn-keeper is looking concerned but he is not saying anything.

But wait - his expression has changed to a brighter one and he is beckoning to us. I am following him and he seems to be taking us behind the inn!

He's pointing to the stable - I don't believe it!

It is all very well for me but Mary and Joseph aren't used to staying in stables - whatever next!

Still, Mary and Joseph have accepted the offer, gratefully, and we are all going in.

It is not bad in here, actually; quite roomy, plenty of fresh hay. There are other animals in here as well; a cow and several oxen. They look a bit puzzled, as well they might, but I will explain the situation to them in a minute.

Joseph has helped Mary off my back and unstrapped the bundle - what a relief! They are both making beds for themselves out of the hay and settling down. The breath from us animals will keep them warm.

Now is there any water? Yes, there is some in the corner. I'll have a drink, then settle myself down too - I really don't feel hungry.

I have never felt so tired.

    Oh, this soft hay is bliss.

        I'll close my eyes and soon............

What was that? It sounded like a baby crying. What ever it was, it has woken me up. Where am I? I don't know this place.

Oh, yes I remember. I am in a stable in Bethlehem. Gosh, the baby - it must have been born in the night, in this stable. How extraordinary! I must have been in a deep sleep because I did not hear a thing.

Oh look! It's beautiful!

Mary and Joseph can't take their eyes off the little mite! Mary has wrapped the baby in a blanket, brought from home, and is using the manger, from where the animals usually eat, as a cradle. What a clever idea!

Shh! I hear footsteps. Someone's coming! Who can it be?

The door is opening and some shepherds are coming in and staring at our baby!

Mary is showing them the baby and telling them it is a boy named Jesus.

The shepherds are kneeling down and seem quite overcome with emotion.

They tell us their tale: while some quietly watched over their flock and others dozed off a scary thing happened.

They saw a beautiful creature who had human features, apart from her shining face, light all around her head and wings. She flew down from the sky to talk to these shepherds on their hillside. She told them to visit the new baby in this stable!

But how did the creature know about our baby, I wonder?

Now the shepherds are leaving, talking excitedly amongst themselves.

Oh, what was that?

I looked up just then and caught sight of something bright through a crack in the stable roof. Let me look again through this window.

It's a star - a very, very bright star, lighting up the sky like no other star has ever done before - a jewel in the sky! It has given me a strange feeling.

Oh, look at the little baby! Isn't he sweet?

I can't wait to give him rides when he grows a bit bigger.

I bet we will be great friends.

Now what? The door is opening again - more visitors!

Oh! I can't believe my eyes.

Just wait till you hear what I can see now - three richly dressed gentlemen each wearing a sort of crown. They must be kings. Well, to have one king visit would be something - but three!

I didn't know all this happened when a baby was born!

The kings are kneeling before Jesus and each is presenting a gift to him - how exciting! The first gift is gold, the most precious of metals! The second is frankincense and the third is myrrh - both lovely smelling substances.

The kings are telling Mary and Joseph that they followed the star to find the baby and it stopped over this stable. I bet that surprised them!

The kings are leaving now. Mary and Joseph are thanking them. As for the baby - he is sound asleep!

What a lovely picture they all make; the proud, happy parents, looking much more relaxed than they did yesterday, watching over their dear, little son as he sleeps peacefully in the manger.

I wonder what life has in store for him?

I suddenly feel so happy, yet tearful - I am a silly, old donkey. All this excitement and yesterday's gruelling journey has made me a tired, old donkey too. I shall sleep again now and dream sweet dreams of my new, little friend.

Every baby born is very special but I think that our baby is the most special of all.

But I suppose I would think that, wouldn't I?

Goodnight!"